Fashion

Kitty

by **Charise Mericle Harper**

SUPER!

Hyperion
Paperbacks
for
Children

New York

Text and illustrations
© 2005 by Charise Mericle Harper
All rights reserved. No part of this book may be reproduced or
transmitted in any form or by any means, electronic or mechanical,
including photocopying, recording, or by any information storage
and retrieval system, without written permission from the publisher.
For information address Hyperion Books for Children,
114 Fifth Avenue, New York, New York 10011-5690.
Printed in Singapore
First Hyperion Paperback Edition
7 9 10 8 6 F850-6835-5 12350
Library of Congress Cataloging-in-Publication Data on file.
ISBN 10: 0-7868-5134-1
ISBN 13: 978-0-7868-5134-8
Visit
www.hyperionbooksforchildren.com

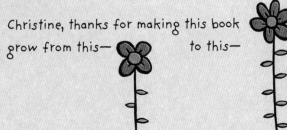

Christine, thanks for making this book
grow from this—   to this—

For Alessandra
for believing
in F.K.
For Ivy
for being
such a girl
For Amy—
my friend
and fan of
great shoes

S.M.

L.H.

This is Kiki Kittie.

She lives with her mother, father, little sister, Lana, and pet mouse named Mousie. The Kittie family is unusual for three reasons:

1 The Kittie family has a pet mouse.

2 Kiki and Lana get to pick out all their own clothes.

3 The Kittie family knows the secret identity of Fashion Kitty.

The **FIRST** reason the Kittie family is unusual is that a cat having a mouse for a pet is similar to a human having a chocolate cake for a pet.

Only, the Kittie family doesn't feel that way about Mousie, because they are vegetarians . . .

4

. . . which means they don't eat meat.

But being unusual means that other cats, even the kittie family's friends and relatives, probably wouldn't feel the same way about Mousie.

I love Mousie burgers!

Mousie snacks! Yum, yum!

I make a good mouse pie.

Even though the Kittie family loves all their friends, they decided to keep Mousie a secret. After all, every family has a few secrets.

Father Kittie built Mousie a special smell-proof clubhouse in the closet in Kiki's room. Any time cats come over, Mousie runs into the clubhouse and locks the door.

But she can't tell anybody Mousie's real name, not even her family, because six months ago...

Which was no big surprise because...

The second reason the Kittie family is unusual is that Mother Kittie believes in free fashion, which means she lets Kiki and Lana pick out all their own clothes. Most mothers don't do this because it upsets them when patterns like:

are displayed all together on one body.

This doesn't bother Mother Kittie. As long as Kiki and Lana wear jackets and hats in the wintertime, Mother Kittie is happy.

Kiki has a natural flair for fashion.
Everyone says so:

Kiki's teacher

She's a creative dresser!

I made up a poem: Should I wear this, yes, or no? Kiki's the one who's sure to know!

Kiki's best friend, June

Even Mother Kittie.

Ready for school, dear?

Oh, that looks nice!

Lana, on the other hand, is a different story. She wears some very unusual clothing combinations.

← STOCKINGS

← UNDERPANTS ON THE OUTSIDE

UNDERSHIRT ON THE OUTSIDE ↓

← STOCKINGS

PANTS TOO BIG →

STOCKINGS

1 SKIRT →

2 SKIRTS →

3 SKIRTS →

Sometimes Kiki just can't help herself and she says:

You're a fashion nightmare!

says Lana, who then runs off to do whatever four-year-olds do.

kiki is glad that Lana doesn't go to school yet. At least at home no one can see her.

says Mother kittie when kiki complains.

But kiki knows that mothers don't always see the truth about their children, and she secretly wonders if sometimes they are too nice.

The **THIRD** and most important reason the kittie family is unusual is that they know the secret identity of Fashion Kitty.

This is Fashion Kitty in her Fashion Hero Pose.

FIGHT FOR FASHION FREEDOM!

Fashion Kitty is a hero to all who struggle with fashion dilemmas.

Sometimes that's not a good thing.

Fashion Kitty doesn't live on top of a mountain,

in a fancy apartment building,

or even in a stylish secret superhero cave.

She lives with her mother, father, and little sister, Lana. That's right! Fashion Kitty is really Kiki Kittie. Kiki wasn't always a fashion hero. Right up until her birthday four months ago, Kiki Kittie was just her regular fashionable self. But on her birthday, something unexplainable happened.

Kiki was blowing out her candles on her birthday cake when a shelf above her broke and sent a pile of fashion magazines tumbling down on her head.

In fact, the list of unfortunate things that happened in the next six seconds is quite long.

the shelf broke when Kiki was directly
underneath it blowing out the candles on
her birthday cake;

the magazines hit Kiki on the head, causing her to fall down and knock over the table that held the birthday cake;

the falling table pushed Lana onto the floor, headfirst into the birthday cake;

Mother Kittie accidentally kicked Father Kittie on the leg when she tried to catch the falling Lana;

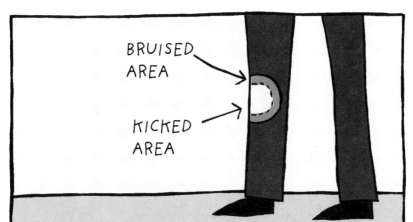

BRUISED
AREA

KICKED
AREA

the leg Mother Kittie kicked already had a big bruise on it from two days before, when Father Kittie had tripped on one of Lana's toys;

Father Kittie, while yelling and grabbing his sore leg, knocked over a prized antique vase that was his and Mrs. Kittie's favorite wedding present;

and the vase broke.

But the most unfortunate thing was that Kiki Kittie was lying very still on the floor, with her eyes closed, and she was not sleeping.

Mother Kittie screamed; Lana screamed; Father Kittie stopped yelling; and then Kiki slowly opened one eye.

Often, when bad things happen, it is comforting to make a silent list of how it could have been worse.

It would have been worse if:
—Kiki had not woken up.
—Lana had hit her head.
—Father Kittie had fallen down.

Looking at the mess, Mother Kittie said:

It's fortunate that no one cut themselves on the broken vase.

It's fortunate that Kiki only has a bump on her head.

It's fortunate that Lana likes chocolate.

And then they laughed, because Lana was covered with chocolate cake.

Later, when everything was almost cleaned up and everyone was getting ready to go out to Tom's Treats, the most fancy and delicious cake-and-ice-cream restaurant in town, Lana said:

It's fortunate that Mousie was on the shelf with the candle

and not the shelf with the magazines.

And everyone agreed it was.

And then, right when everything seemed almost normal, the unexplainable thing happened. Kiki screamed and fell to the floor. Mother and Father Kittie rushed over, thinking the same horrible thought:

Oh, no! She's dying!

In fact, Kiki was just fine, except that she wasn't Kiki anymore. When she stood up she was . . .

I'm off to fight for free fashion!

said Fashion Kitty, and she flew out the door, leaving Mother and Father Kittie, Lana, and even Mousie standing there with their mouths open.

Super Abilities of Fashion Kitty

Brain that can mix and match hundreds of outfits in a second

Ears that hear the distress call of someone in need of fashion help

X-ray eyes that can see through buildings or anything else that's in the way

Heart, mostly good

Tail of comfort. One touch of the tail makes everything seem all right

Supersonic feet that make Fashion Kitty really bounce

She flew down to a house, hopped in the window, and landed on the carpet in front of a very startled Mary Jane Tabby.

Fashion Kitty had to explain herself again. When you are just starting out as a fashion hero, things aren't so easy.

NO! Faux pas means big mistake. I'm here to help you. If you wear that outfit to school tomorrow, it will be a big mistake!

But Priscilla Persian, the most popular kitty in school, gave me a secret note that said all her friends were going to wear polka-dotted shorts over their pants tomorrow.

She's never given me a note before... ...or even talked to me,

and she's popular and fashionable. I'd like her to be my friend.

Fashion Kitty thought about the situation and chose her words carefully.

Priscilla Persian is a horrible, spoiled, mean kitty!

super

cute

kitty

extra

- -

swanky

- -

look

one

---

sweet

---

getup

look at that

---

cool

---

fashionista

what a

---

styling

---

trendsetter

now, that's a

- -

fancy

- -

ensemble

check out the

---

hip

---

outfit

Sometimes a kitty just needs a friend to say it.

Isn't it fun to try something new?

It sure is!

It's like having a whole new wardrobe.

Of course, Mary Jane didn't want Fashion Kitty to leave. It's always fun to have an expert pay lots of attention to you.

Mary Jane, my job here is done. I must go!

Don't forget, you're still the same great Mary Jane!

In a new package.

Fashion Kitty flew up to Priscilla Persian's bedroom window and climbed in.

Priscilla was a slave to fashion magazines.

OOOHHH!

That means she didn't have her own style.

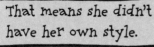

She just copied whatever she saw.

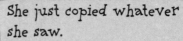

Perfect!

Fashion Kitty took all Priscilla's unread fashion magazines and drew dark circles aound the fashion models' eyes.

This will do the trick!

WOW

It wasn't a nice thing to do, but then, Priscilla wasn't a very nice kitty.

I'll put these next to her bed so she'll read them in the morning.

Serves her right!

Hugga, hugga, hrrr, hugga, hugga . . .

Lana was in the kitchen eating ice cream and smashed cake,

and Mother and Father Kittie were looking up superheroes on the Internet,

when Kiki walked in the front door.

Hello?

As soon as Mother and Father Kittie saw her, they asked all the important "W" and "H" questions.

Where have you been?
What was that?

When did you learn to fly?

Why did you leave?

Oh, honey! Are you okay?
How did that happen?

I don't know!

answered Kiki, and she began to cry. Her head hurt, and she wasn't sure she wanted to be a fashion hero.

Father Kittie put Lana to bed,

and then he and Mother Kittie sat with Kiki while she ate ice cream and three pieces of new birthday cake.

She was surprisingly hungry.

57

But Kiki just rubbed her lumpy head and said:

You aren't supposed to tell what you wish for or it won't come true.

Did you wish you could fly?

Can you do it again?

Can I have a piece of cake?

asked Lana, who was standing in the doorway.

You can put Lana to bed, but you can't make her stay there,

sighed Mother Kittie.

said Kiki.

This was a very unusual thing for Kiki to say. It wasn't like her to be generous with Lana; but then this had been an unusual day.

Mother and Father Kittie looked at each other

and quietly raised their eyebrows.

This is something adults do when they want to say, "Hey, look at that, isn't that nice?" but don't want their children to hear it.

Can I have a piece of new cake?

Lana was full of questions and her mouth was full of chocolate cake, but Mother Kittie didn't say anything about chewing with your mouth open. On a normal day she would have.

Kiki wasn't sure why she felt she should keep her adventures as Fashion Kitty a secret.

She was too tired to talk about it anyway.

said Lana. And with that, the whole family went right to bed without washing their faces or brushing their teeth . . . It was that kind of day.

whispered Kiki to Mousie, and she mumbled words like:

stripes   polka dots   and checks

until she fell asleep.

The next morning, while the family was eating breakfast and Kiki was opening her birthday presents from the day before, Kiki said:

I'm making a Fashion Kitty costume today.

Don't you have to go to school?

NICE SHIRT IN BOX

Well, just this once, why don't we let Kiki stay at home with us,

said Mother Kittie.

Kiki spent the day trying various costume looks.

Lana, of course, had an opinion about everything.

You look mean.

Kiki didn't pay any attention to her until Lana said:

You look like that clown we saw at the circus...

Well, not quite.

Or maybe . . .

a giant beach ball!

LEAVE ME ALONE!

yelled Kiki. She couldn't help herself. After all, a kitty can only take so much.

Lana looked upset for about five seconds, then she said:

Fashion Kitty is a lot nicer than you!

Then she skipped off, singing a song that only a four-year-old would like.

Fashion Kitty is my friend. La, la, la.

Kiki quickly changed out of the beach-ball outfit, and after only twenty minutes more of fashion work, had a costume she was happy with.

asked Mother Kitty, looking at Kiki's flashy new costume. Mothers are always ready for new things, but having your daughter turn into a fashion hero is not one of them.

said Kiki, because she knew it would happen again, and it would be very soon . . .

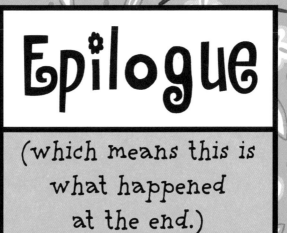

Epilogue

(which means this is
what happened
at the end.)

Early the next morning, Priscilla Persian looked at her magazines as soon as she got up.

Wow!
These circles around the eyes must be the latest eye look.

She picked out her outfit for the day.

It's so hard to decide: which fabulous outfit should I wear?

What have you done to your eyes? Go and wash that off immediately!

I can't. I used permanent marker.

After breakfast, Priscilla walked to school.

Outside, in the school yard, she met her friend Sally.

Priscilla ran screaming
into the bathroom.

The End

Coming soon . . .

Fashion Kitty

versus
the Fashion Queen